For Oliver

*There are days when Bartholomew is naughty,
and other days when he is very, very good.*

Copyright © 2001 by Virginia Miller

All rights reserved.

First U.S. edition 2001

Library of Congress Cataloging-in-Publication Data

Miller, Virginia.
In a minute! / Virginia Miller — 1st U.S. ed.
p.   cm.
Summary: Bartholomew wants to play with George, who is always too busy doing chores, but when
George is ready to play, Bartholomew has his own ideas about what he wants to do.
ISBN 0-7636-1270-7
[1. Bears — Fiction. 2. House cleaning — Fiction. 2. Play — Fiction.] I. Title.
PZ7.M6373 In 2000
[E] — dc21   99-058228

Printed in Belgium

This book was typeset in Garamond.
The illustrations were done in soft pencil and colored markers.

Candlewick Press
2067 Massachusetts Avenue
Cambridge, Massachusetts 02140

IN A MINUTE!

Virginia Miller

CANDLEWICK PRESS
CAMBRIDGE, MASSACHUSETTS

George was carrying firewood.
Bartholomew wanted to play.
"In a minute, Ba," said George.
"When I finish, then
we'll play."

George was hanging out the
laundry. Bartholomew wanted to play.
"In a minute, Ba," said George.
"I'm busy now. In a minute,
then we'll play."

George was sweeping.
Bartholomew got in the way.
He wanted to play.

"IN A

MINUTE!"

George said in a big voice.
"Wait until I finish."

Bartholomew waited and waited.
He waited and he waited.

George was very busy.

Then at last, George finished his chores.
"I can play now, Ba," he said.

"What shall we play? On the swing . . . ?
With your toys . . . ? I know, hide-and-seek!"

"Nah, nah, nah," said Bartholomew.

Bartholomew got his little red wagon
and took George to the woodpile.
He wanted to play . . .
carrying firewood.

He wanted to play . . .
bringing in the laundry.

He wanted to play . . . sweeping the floor.

"Played enough now, Ba?" George asked.

"Nah!" said Bartholomew.

George got the picnic basket.
"Shall we have our picnic now," he asked,
"or in a minute?"

"Nah!" said Bartholomew.

So George and Bartholomew
had their picnic.

"What a busy day we've had," said George.
"You've been such a help, Ba.
Why don't we have a little rest now
and we'll . . . clear up . . . in a . . ."